A LIFT-THE-FLAP BOOK

Emily and Her Baby-Sitter

Claire Masurel • Illustrated by Susan Calitri

PUFFIN BOOKS

Emily's parents are going out.
The baby-sitter is coming over.
"I hear the doorbell," says Dad.

Mom and Dad kiss
Emily good-bye.

"See you later!"

"Let's make a house for your little bunny," says Laura.

"Now we can have a snack," says Laura.

Emily likes to play
hide-and-seek.

"Ready or not,
here I come,"
says Laura.

It's almost time for bed.
Laura helps Emily get the bath ready.

Laura reads Emily a story.